To Chloe,
May all your Christmas wishes come true!

Love....................................

Chloe is *excited*
Christmastime is here!

December

3

December

1

She says, "I wish for lots and lots of fluffy snow this year!"

Chloe writes to Santa.
The letter takes her ages.

"Perhaps I've wished for way too much..."
(There are over 50 pages!)

Dear Santa,

Chloe decorates the tree
with twinkly lights that glow.

Christmas
decorations

Look at Chloe up on stage.
She's in the Christmas play.

She wished to make
her family proud and
have the greatest day!

The kitchen's very busy.
Chloe can smell baking.

"I wish that I could eat that bowl of cake mix Dad is making."

Chloe wakes at 5 a.m.
"It's Christmas Day!
Yippee!"

She runs downstairs
to find a pile of
presents beneath
the tree.

This jumper's really **itchy**.
She tries to grin and bear it,
but Chloe really wishes that
she didn't have to wear it!

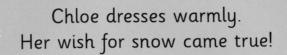

Chloe dresses warmly.
Her wish for snow came true!

She's off to build a snowman now.
Perhaps she can build two!

Chloe's sledging down the hill. "I wish I could *speed* up!"

Her wish comes true,
her sledge is *fast*
when powered by a pup!

It's after Christmas dinner,
and everyone is snoring.
Chloe says to her best friend,
"I wish it was less **BORING!**"

Later, Mum asks Chloe,
"Did your **BIGGEST** wish come true?"
"Oh yes," she smiles,
"that wish was being…"

" …here with **all** of you!"

Do you wish for fun with friends,
or a family trip that never ends?
Whatever it is that you hold dear,
keep your Christmas wishes here!

I wish...
It will
snow on
Christmas.

I wish...
everone
will be good
at Christmas
time.

I wish
I will get
the LOL house
for
Christmas.

I wish
Santa will
make Katie
be nice.

Written by J. D. Green
Illustrated by Julia Seal

Copyright © Hometown World Ltd 2018
Hometown World Ltd
1 Queen Street
Bath
BA1 1HE

www.hometownworld.co.uk

Follow us @hometownworldbooks

ISBN 978-1-78553-942-8
All rights reserved
Printed in Italy
HTW_PO201806

put **me** in the **story**®

Bestselling books starring your child!
www.putmeinthestory.co.uk

SANTA
STOP
HERE!